GOD'S LITTLE HOUSE

A Picture Book by
SANDOL STODDARD

Illustrated by Jana Winthers Newman

To Maggie Ross

Many long years ago I was a child
Lost in the woods; the night was dark
   and wild.

I saw a light at last, and ran to it,

And there was a tiny house all brightly lit;

And in the house was sitting, still as stone,

A little old, old woman all alone.

"So you have found me," she said,
  looking pleased.

I tried to answer, but instead,
  I sneezed.

"God bless you!" cried the hermit,
  jumping up.

She brought me bread, and hot
  soup in a cup,

And quickly took my shoes and
    put them by
The fire, and rubbed my feet till
    they were dry.

"Some people think," she said,
"it's very odd

That I live here alone and talk
with God."

"What do you think?" she asked, but
   all I said

Was, "Please, I think I'd like to
   go to bed."

She tucked me in, and I slept till dawn
was coming,

And all night at her loom I heard
her humming

A song that was like weaving or like spinning;

It had no words, nor ending, nor beginning.

And when the sun was up, I took
    the broom

And swept the corners of her one
    small room,

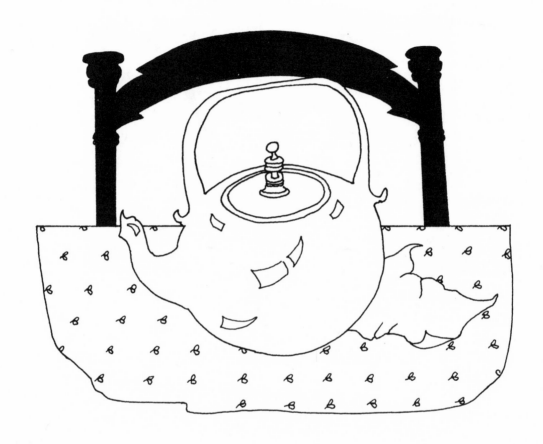

And polished up her kettle, and
  chopped wood,

And filled her tiny stove as best
  I could.

"God bless you!" once again I heard
    her say.

"And will you leave this place or
    will you stay

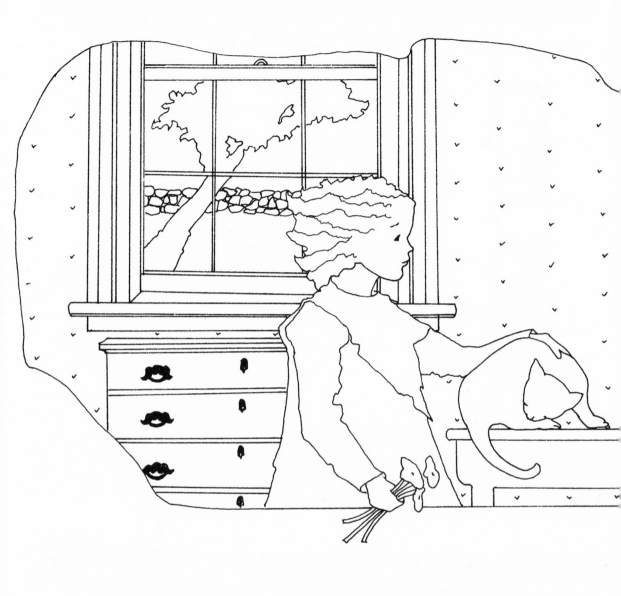

For a third blessing? Now you have
   had two,

I know another that may come to you."

And as I stood there wondering,
    I heard

Upon her windowsill a little bird

Singing the same song I had heard
   before;

I thought I loved that music more
   and more.

And so I stayed, and learned a
 hermit's ways:

She taught me how to heal and pray
 and praise

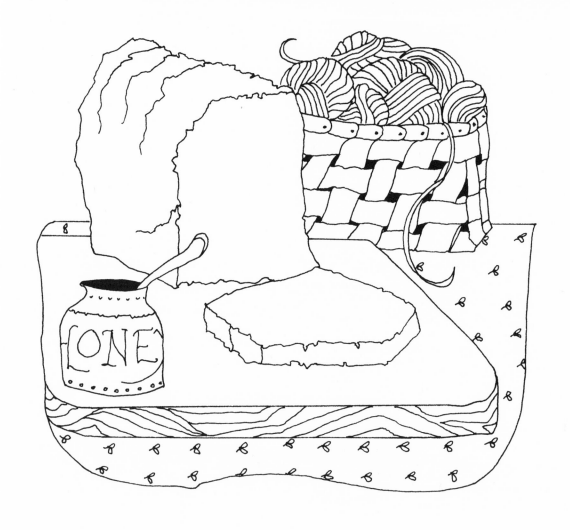

God's holy name, and how to spin
   a thread

And weave a garment warm, and
   bake good bread.

But when I asked her, "Teach me
   about God!"

She only smiled, and gave a
   little nod,

And never said a word. What could I do?
She did not want to tell me what
    she knew.

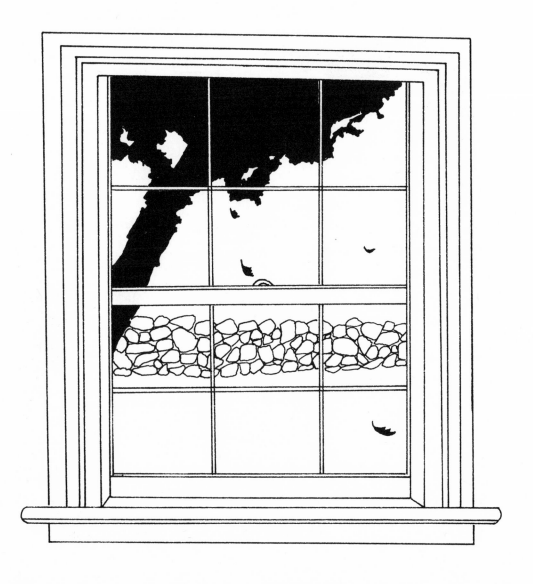

Thus time went by until my quiet friend
Had grown so old, her life came
    to its end.

She went to heaven with a shining face,
And I stayed here alone to keep
her place.

My hair is white now, and the ceiling's
    taller--

Or is it only that my body's smaller?

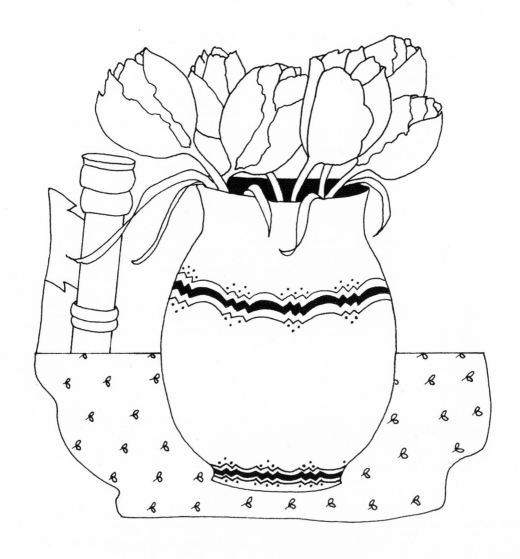

And still I have not heard the third
   "God bless"

Although I do not lack for happiness.

So I sit here, this wild and stormy night
Beside the window, all my lamps
    alight,

Saying my prayers, doing my usual mending,

Humming the old song that has no ending,

And here are some words for it
that I am making:

O heart that hungers, all is here
for the taking:

God is in the fire, in the warm
bread baking,

God is in the song we hear,
sleeping or waking,

God is in the little house filled
   beyond measure

With every need and every good
   pleasure,

And a lost child is God's dearest
   treasure.

But hark! There is a knock upon
 my door;

I will hear tonight the blessing
 I've waited for.

Come in, my child. Why, you are
wet all through!
So, you have found me--
God bless you!